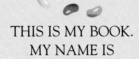

THIS IS MY BOOK.
MY NAME IS

_____

# Disney's
## THE
# LION KING

# Simba's
# Daring Rescue

Adapted by Andrea Posner-Sanchez

Illustrated by Don Williams

Random House 🏠 New York

Copyright © 1996, 2001 by Disney Enterprises, Inc. All rights reserved under International and Pan-American Copyright Conventions.
Published in the United States by Random House, Inc., New York, and simultaneously in Canada by Random House of Canada Limited, Toronto,
in conjunction with Disney Enterprises, Inc. Originally published in a different form as *The Cave Monster* by Golden Books Publishing Company, Inc., in 1996.

Library of Congress Catalog Card Number: 00-110034    ISBN: 0-7364-1177-1

www.randomhouse.com/kids/disney

Printed in the United States of America    June 2001    10 9 8 7 6 5 4 3 2 1

JELLYBEAN BOOKS, RANDOM HOUSE, and the Random House colophon are registered trademarks,
and the Jellybean Books colophon is a trademark of Random House, Inc.

One day Simba and Nala went for a walk in the forest. Zazu flew overhead to keep an eye on the curious cubs.

Soon the young lions came upon a dark cave they had never seen before.

"Since I'm going to be the Lion King, I should be the ruler of this cave," Simba declared. "And I say I'm the only one allowed inside!"

Nala didn't think that sounded fair.

"You can't stop me!" she said as she walked toward the entrance to the cave.

Simba leaped on top of her, and the two cubs began wrestling.

"I want to see what's in there!" Nala said as she flipped Simba over her shoulder.

Simba landed on the ground with a **PLOP**.

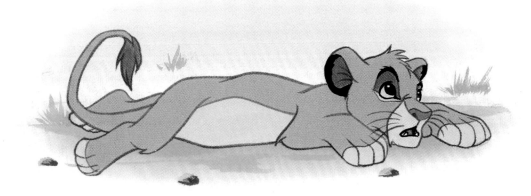

As Simba scrambled to his feet, he heard a noise coming from inside the cave.

Zazu started to worry. "Perhaps it's best if no one goes in there," said the cautious bird. But Simba was curious.

Nala, Simba, and Zazu all listened as the noise got louder and **LOUDER** and **LOUDER**. Zazu nervously backed away.

Simba began to get scared. It sounded as if a giant monster with twenty feet was stomping around the cave!

But Nala wasn't frightened at all. "Since you're too much of a scaredy-cat, I'm going inside," she told Simba.

Before Simba could say anything, Nala crept into the deep, dark cave. When the tip of Nala's tail slipped out of sight, Simba heard a very loud scream. *"Aaagh!"*

Simba rushed to save Nala but stopped short when he spotted two eyes glowing from the back of the cave. Then Simba heard a deep voice.

"Who dares to disturb me?" the voice demanded.

Simba tried to sound fearless as he answered. "It is I, Simba, the future Lion King. And I'm with Zazu, the king's minister."

"Ha!" shouted the voice. "I'm not afraid of you or your feathered friend. And I can tie a knot in the king's tail!"

Zazu's feathers shook with fright. "I'd better summon the king!" he said, and flew off.

Simba was truly frightened, but he knew he
had to rescue his friend. He raced into the narrow
cave and saw Nala pressed against the wall.

She was pointing toward the back of the cave.
"It's horrible!" she whimpered. Nala and Simba
both jumped at the sound of Nala's voice. The echo
inside the cave made her sound like the monster!

Just then a tiny spider crawled in front of Simba.

"Are you the monster?" asked Simba in amazement.

"I was only trying to defend myself," the spider said meekly. "It's scary being so small."

Simba and Nala laughed in relief. Both cubs realized they didn't need to be scared of something that was just as scared of them.

Finally, Mufasa and Zazu arrived at the cave.
The king let out a mighty **ROAR**!

"Come out and defend yourself!" said the Lion King.
"I have come to save my son and his best friend."

"We don't need any help," Simba told his father as
he trotted out of the cave.

"I saved Nala all by myself."

"My son, the hero," Mufasa said proudly. "Let me take a look at this monster you've conquered."

Mufasa stared at the little spider. "This is the
monster who claims he can tie my tail in a knot?"
The Lion King couldn't help laughing. "Well, it
looks as if we have a little hero *and* a little monster."

"Now *I* need a hero to protect me from that awful bird," begged the spider as he spotted Zazu. "Please don't let him eat me."

"Blech!" said Zazu. "Just the thought is sickening."

Simba playfully swatted Zazu with his tail. "Stay
back, you awful bird. No one eats this spider while
I'm around!"

Mufasa smiled. "Zazu is not a threat, but others may be," he told Simba. "Heroes always take care of those who need help. You must find a way to protect the spider."

Simba thought a bit. "Let's tell everyone you rule this cave," he said to his father. "Then no one will dare harm anything inside it!"

"Zazu will announce it to the kingdom," said Mufasa as he led the cubs away.

"Good-bye," yelled the spider. "Heroes are always welcome here!"

Jellybean Books®

**Is your child ready to read?**
**Move on up to Step into Reading® Books!**